The Case
of the
Hiccupping
Ears

Tommy Nelson® Books by Bill Myers

Series

The Incredible Worlds of
Wally McDoogle

Picture Book
Baseball for Breakfast

www.Billmyers.com

SECRET AGENT DINGLEDORF
... and his trusty dog, SPLAT

The Case of the Hiccupping Ears

BILL MYERS

Illustrations
Meredith Johnson

www.tommynelson.com

A Division of Thomas Nelson, Inc.
www.ThomasNelson.com

THE CASE OF THE HICCUPPING EARS

Text copyright © 2003 by Bill Myers
Illustrations by Meredith Johnson. Copyright © 2003 by Tommy
Nelson®, a Division of Thomas Nelson, Inc.

Published in Nashville, Tennessee, by Tommy Nelson®, a Division
of Thomas Nelson, Inc.

Library of Congress Cataloging-in-Publication Data

Myers, Bill, 1953–
     The case of the hiccupping ears / Bill Myers ; illustrations
Meredith Johnson.
          p. cm. — (Secret Agent Dingledorf . . . and his trusty dog,
          Splat; 5)
     Summary: Ten-year-old secret agent Bernie Dingledorf flies
into action when the boys of B.A.D.D. try to take over the
world again, this time by mixing up brain waves and causing
the bodies of children and teens to do weird things.
     ISBN: 1-4003-0178-5 (pbk.)
     [1. Brainwashing—Fiction. 2. Body, Human—Fiction.
3. Spies—Fiction. 4. Humorous stories.] I. Johnson,
Meredith, ill. II. Title.
PZ7.M98234 Car 2003
[Fic]—dc22   2003015482

Printed in the United States of America

05 06 07 RRD 6 5

For Jonathan—
a man who walks his talk.

*"I am fearfully
and wonderfully made."*

Psalm 139:14 (NIV)

Contents

CHAPTER 1

The Case Begins . . .

Life with my three older sisters is weird.

But this morning their weirdness was weirder than their normal weirdness.

Sound weird?

It was.

It all started at breakfast. . . . Mom had the radio blaring with weird music as everybody ran around the kitchen talking and eating.

Everybody including Sister 1. Better known as . . .

THE PROM QUEEN

"Brad is, like, *soooo* cute. And Tommy is,

like, *soooo* sweet. I just don't know which one I want to ask me out to the . . ."

I'll spare you the rest of her chatter. Let's just say the only time she's not talking about boys is when she's thinking about boys. And the only time she's not thinking about boys is when she's sleeping (though I guess she still dreams about them).

But her boy talk wasn't the weird part. The weird part was her shoving a warm waffle into her ear! (How's that for an eating disorder?)

I thought of asking her about it. But as her little brother, I knew it wouldn't do any good. (Pond scum gets more respect than little brothers.)

Still, her weirdness was nothing compared to the cell-phone weirdness of Sister 2. Better known as . . .

THE GOSSIP QUEEN

". . . what Billy said Bonnie said about Bobby when Buddy said . . ."

But the weirdness wasn't *what* she gossiped. It was *how* she gossiped.

She didn't have her ear pressed to the receiver. She had her nose pressed to it! That's right. She was trying to listen to the phone with her nose!

But the award for real weirdness went to Sister 3. Better known as . . .

THE FASHION QUEEN

"Do you think this top makes me look fat? Are these shoes waaay too last month? What about . . ."

And what's so weird about that, you ask?

Instead of eating with her mouth, she was stuffing a banana up her nose!

It was more than I could stand.

"Why is everyone acting so weird?" I shouted.

Nobody answered.

I tried another question. "What's going on?"

Repeat in the *No Answer Department*.

Then I discovered the reason: I wasn't shouting with my mouth. It was sealed tight. Instead, I was trying to shout through my eyeballs!

Like I said, things were pretty weird.

Unfortunately, the weirdness only got weirder when I headed to school. . . .

I was barely outside the door when I heard:

"Hey, Bernie *(sniff, sniff)*, wait up!"

I turned to see I.Q., my best friend. He did his usual sniffing and pushing up of his glasses. But he was also doing something else.

Instead of walking on his feet, he was rolling on his side!

"What are you doing?" I shouted.

Actually, that's what I wanted to shout. But since I was still trying to talk with my eyelids, the only thing that came out was

"blink, blink
blink, blink, blink."

"Hey, guys!"

We turned to see Priscilla. She's my

other best friend, even if she is a girl . . . and pretty. But don't tell her that, unless you like getting beat up. (She has a black belt in karate.)

I was glad to see she wasn't rolling on the sidewalk like I.Q.

I would have been gladder, if she hadn't been walking on her hands . . . and hiccupping through her ears!

Suddenly, Splat the Wonder-dog raced from my porch after us.

"Woof! Woof!"

He looked a little worried.

Not that I blamed him. He seemed to be the only one acting normal.

That was the good news.

Unfortunately, with Splat, there's always some bad news.

"BLINK, BLINK!
BLINK, BLINK, BLINK!"

I shouted.

(*Translation:* "SPLAT, LOOK OUT FOR THAT CAR!")

Splat looked up just in time to see a car bounce up on our sidewalk.

A normal dog would have jumped out of the way.

(Unfortunately, Splat is about fifty pounds over normal.)

He tried to leap, but his leaper was overloaded.

Then, at the last second,

SCREECH! SQUEAL!

the car swerved off the sidewalk. It missed Splat and drove onto our front lawn.

And it kept right on going until it

K-Smash-ed

into our front porch.
Priscilla raced to the car on her hands.

"Mister! Mister!" she yelled.

I.Q. rolled forward. "Are you all right?" he asked.

I ran toward it. *"Blink! Blink! Blink, blink!"* I blinked.

The car door opened. The same music

that had been blasting from Mom's radio was blasting from the car's speakers.

The good news was, the teenage driver wasn't hurt.

The bad news was, he'd been sitting on his head and driving with his feet!

Suddenly, my thoughtful thinker thought a thoughtful thought.

(*Translation:* I figured things were getting weirder.)

And, by the looks of things, I couldn't have been more right. . . .

CHAPTER 2

School Daze

The only thing weirder than walking to school was being at school!

We had barely entered the building before we heard that strange music again. It blasted through the hallways. Someone was playing it through the PA system.

But what we heard was nothing compared to what we saw. Some of the kids were rolling on their sides like I.Q. Others were walking on their hands like Priscilla.

And the rest?

They were either cartwheeling, back-flipping, or somersaulting their way down the hall. (Which was okay, I suppose. Until

you got to the stairs. Something about
somersaulting down stairs

BOUNCE—"OOOUUCH!"
        BOUNCE—"OOOUUCH!"
                BOUNCE—"EEEECH!"

looked kinda painful.)
But not as painful as when they stopped
bouncing and started

    K-SLAM
            K-SLAM
                    K-SLAM-ing

into the wall at the bottom of those stairs.
But the weirdness didn't stop with them
moving through the halls.
Kids with colds were

"Aн—CHOOO!!!"-ing

through their ears.

Girls with hairbrushes were combing their teeth.

And those little first graders with that disgusting nose-picking habit? Well, their habit didn't change, just their method. Now they picked their noses with their toes.

Repeat after me:

"EWWWWWWWWW!"
(very good)

Yes sir, things were definitely weird.

But it looked like the mix-ups only affected kids and not grown-ups. Which explains why Mrs. Hooplesnort kept trying to teach health class.

"Class," she yelled. "Class, be seated!"

Everyone obeyed and sat on their knees, their shoulders, their stomachs, and, of course, their heads.

"I'm not sure why you insist on mixing everything up," she shouted. "After all, the human body is a wonderful creation just the way it is."

Everyone agreed by nodding their elbows, their ankles, or their kneecaps.

She continued. "The head was designed to be at the top of the body so we can see greater distances. Feet are designed for walking. And we have two for balance."

More elbow, ankle, and kneecap nodding.

"And do you know why we were given two eyes instead of one?"

Raymond the human rash (he's always got some kind of skin problem) had an answer. But instead of raising his hand, he raised his tongue.

"Yes, Raymond?"

He shoved his hand under his armpit and answered with those gross hand-under-the-armpit noises.

"Burpa-burpa-burpa-burpa."

"That's right," Mrs. Hooplesnort said, pretending to understand. "Two eyes allow us to tell if things are close or far. In fact, shut one eye and try touching your finger-tips together."

We tried, and she was right. It was hard to perfectly touch them.

We all showed our surprise by

"*click, click, click*"-ing

our teeth and

"*knock, knock, knock*"-ing

our knees. And, of course, the ever popular

"*wiggle, wiggle, wiggle*"-ing

of our ears.

(Which, you may notice, is just as successful as talking by blinking your eyelids.)

"And look at your hands," she continued. "Imagine missing something as simple as your thumb. In fact, try picking up something without using your thumb."

We all tried and, sure enough, it was hard.

"So, as you can see, our bodies are wonderfully made, and we should use them the way they were—"

beep-beep-beep-beep

She cleared her throat and tried again. "So, as you can see, we have wonderful bodies that—"

beep-beep-beep-beep

She looked over at me. "Uh, Bernie?" she asked.

"Blink," I blinked.

"I believe that's your underwear ringing."

I nodded, lowered my head, and blinked at my underwear.

But it did not answer.

I tried again. *"Blink, blink!"*

Again, no answer. Just another

beep-beep-beep-beep.

"Aren't you going to answer it?" she asked.

I looked up at her and blinked.

"Well, go ahead."

I blinked at my underwear again. But the results were the same.

She raised her voice and shouted, "Hello? Is anybody there?"

"Agent Dingledorf?" a voice yelled from my underwear.

"No, this is his teacher, Mrs. Hooplesnort. Who is this?"

"This is Big Guy. Where is Secret Agent Dingledorf?"

"He's right here, but—"

"Is he trying to talk with his eyelids?" Big Guy asked.

"Yes, how did you—"

"Well, at least he's not making gross armpit noises."

"Yes, but how—"

"Tell him to come to Headquarters immediately."

"Yes, but—"

"The fate of the world hangs in the balance."

"Excuse me," she called. "Do you always interrupt people when they're trying to talk to—"

"Yes!" he shouted. "Now hurry!"

CHAPTER 3

Mrs. Hooplesnort to the Rescue!

"**B**ernie!" Mrs. Hooplesnort shouted. "They want you to go to Headquarters!"

I looked at her and blinked.

"But how?" she yelled. "Where?"

"Blink, blink!" I blinked.

"Can't you speak?!"

I tried, but nothing happened. Just more blinking.

"What do we do?"

I motioned to the backpack under my desk. It's the one Headquarters gave me. It has all sorts of supercool gizmos inside.

"Your backpack?" she asked. "You want

me to open your backpack?"

"*Blink,*" I blinked.

She quickly

un-*zipppp*-ed

the top and reached inside.

She pulled out a yellow bath toy that

squeaka-squeak-ed.

She looked at me. "A yellow ducky?" she asked. "How's a yellow ducky going to help?"

I pointed to the writing on the side. It read:

Instructions
Turn on by shouting your name.

"Am I supposed to shout my name at it?" she asked.

I nodded and blinked.

She raised the duck to her face. Now they were beak to beak. (I'd say nose-to-beak, but you haven't seen Mrs. Hooplesnort's nose.)

Then she shouted into its face: "MY NAME IS GERTRUDE HOOPLESNORT!"

Nothing happened. (Well, except for the kids giggling at her first name.)

So she tried again: "MY NAME IS GERTRUDE MYRTLE HOOPLESNORT!"

More of nothing. (Except for the giggling over her middle name.)

Suddenly, a bright red sign flashed on the duck's side.

It read:

NAME UNKNOWN. NAME UNKNOWN.
NAME UNKNOWN. NAME UNKNOWN.

I gave Mrs. Hooplesnort a puzzled look.

But she already knew the solution. She raised Ducky Dude to her face and shouted: "MY NAME IS BERNIE DINGLEDORF!"

Suddenly, it

K-POOOOOSH . . .

began to inflate.

She dropped it onto the floor.

We all watched in amazement as it grew to the size of a small rubber raft— complete with bench seats and a great CD sound system.

But this was no ordinary rubber raft complete with bench seats and a great CD sound system. At the back was a powerful rocket engine. A powerful rocket engine that suddenly fired up and

ROARRR-ed

to life.

It also . . .

—blew papers all over the room.

—burned a hole in the back wall.

—and, worst of all worsts, it caused the girls to scream, "It's messing up our hair! It's messing up our hair!"

"WHAT DO WE DO?!" Mrs. Hooplesnort shouted over the roar.

I really get tired of saving the world, but I know somebody has to do it. So I grabbed my backpack, stepped into the raft, and looked over the control panel.

Then I spotted a sign that read:

Instructions
Speak destination into microphone.

I blinked at it.

Nothing.

I blinked again.

Mrs. Hooplesnort joined me in the raft.

"What'd it say?" she shouted.

I pointed at the instructions.

She read them. Then she yelled into the microphone:

"GET US AS FAR FROM
HERE AS POSSIBLE!"

Not exactly the instructions I would
have yelled. But . . .

The rocket grew louder and, suddenly, we

VAA-RRROOOOM-ed

out the door and down the hall.
  Next we

K-RASH-ed

through the front doors of the school.
  Mrs. Hooplesnort sat in front as we
raced down the sidewalk.

"AHHHHHHHH!"

she screamed.
  I sat in the back.

"BLINKKKKKK!"

I blinked.

Up ahead, I spotted Splat, the Wonder-dog. He was waiting faithfully for me to get out of school.

"BLINK BLINK!" I shouted. *"BLINK BLINK!"*

(*Translation:* "LOOK OUT! LOOK OUT!")

But it did no good.

He tried to leap out of the way. But like I said, his leaper was a little overloaded. So, he jumped, and we

SPLAT

hit him. (Well, now you know how he got his name.)

The good news was, he leaped high enough to miss Ducky Dude.

The bad news was, he didn't leap high enough to miss Mrs. Hooplesnort.

"Mwet mhem mwof mee!" she shouted. "Mwet mhem mwof mee!"

(That's supposed to be "Get him off me! Get him off me!" But it's hard talking with a face full of Wonder-dog.)

So, there we were in a rubber raft, racing down the sidewalk. Mrs. Hooplesnort was screaming her head off while I was blinking my eyelids off.

Could things get any worse?

Unfortunately, as you probably know, the answer was a big, fat:

YES!

Super-pooch clung to Mrs. Hooplesnort's face with his front paws. But his back paws were kicking away. Unfortunately, they were kicking away at the switches on the control panel.

No problem. Well, except for that one switch he kicked.

The one labeled:

WARNING

Kick only if you want to go to the moon.

Yes, I'm afraid that's exactly what it said.

Which means, I'm afraid, that's exactly where we

KWOOOOOSHHH

went!

CHAPTER 4

To the Moon . . .

Actually, traveling to the moon wasn't as bad as I thought it would be.

Well, except for the international space station we nearly hit—

"LOOK OUT!" Mrs. Hooplesnort shouted.

"BARK! BARK!" Splat barked.

"BLINK! BLINK!" I blinked.

WHOOOOOSH!
WHOOOOOSH!

the space station *whoosh*-ed.

The good news was, we missed it.

The bad news was, we didn't miss the meteor right behind it.

"LOOK OUT!"

"BARK! BARK!"

"BLINK! BLINK!"

SQUISH! BOING!
whirl-whirl-whirl

(You probably know this, but *SQUISH! BOING!* are the sounds a rubber raft makes when it hits a meteor. And *whirl-whirl-whirl* is the sound it makes when it's *whirl-whirl-whirl*-ing out of control!)

So, there we were, spinning around and around, doing what we do best:

"LOOK OUT! LOOK OUT!" "BARK! BARK!" "BLINK! BLINK!" "LOOK OUT!"

Oh, yeah, there was one other little problem.

Being in outer space meant we had no air to breathe.

NO AIR TO BREATHE?!

(Sorry, I didn't mean to yell. Especially when we have no air to breathe.)

Luckily, I noticed another switch on the control panel that read:

WARNING
Press only if you want to breathe.

I reached past Mrs. Hooplesnort and hit the switch.

Suddenly, three pills appeared. On them was more writing.

DIRECTIONS
Swallow only if you want to breathe.

It seemed like a pretty good idea. So we each popped one into our mouths and, sure enough, we could breathe.

Great, now we could continue with all of our

"LOOK OUT! LOOK OUT!"-ing
"BARK! BARK!"-ing
and
"BLINK! BLINK!"-ing.

It was great fun. But all good things must come to an end.

Before we knew it, or went totally hoarse from the screaming and barking (or blind from the blinking), we

K-POOF!

hit the moon.

Fortunately, it was covered in thick dust, which softened our fall (and explains the *K-POOF!*).

Unfortunately, it was covered in thick dust, which explains Splat's sudden attack of the

"*AH—CHOOO!*"-s.

No problem, except when Splat sneezes, he also sprays. And not just a little. More like a pop can that's been opened after being shaken for three minutes.

"Ick!" Mrs. Hooplesnort complained as she wiped her face.

"Sorry," I said, wiping my own face. "He's allergic to dust."

"Bernie," she shouted, "you're talking?"

"*AH—CHOOO!*"

Splat sneezed in excitement.

They were right. I was using my mouth again. But why? What made the difference?

Mrs. Hooplesnort noticed something else. "Listen," she said.

The rocket had run out of fuel, and now everything was silent.

"I don't hear a thing," I said.

"Exactly!" She grinned. "That strange music is gone."

I listened again. She was right. For the first time that day, I didn't hear the weird music.

"That must be it!" she shouted. "Somehow the music is messing up children's brain waves. It makes them forget how to use their bodies!"

"Yes," I said. I felt my mouth and was grateful to use it again.

"Now you remember how!" she exclaimed.

I nodded.

Again, Splat

"*AH-CHOOO!*"-ed

in excitement.

"We just have one more problem," Mrs. Hooplesnort said, wiping her face.

"How not to drown in doggie drool?" I asked.

She shook her head. "How to get home."

She looked up at the earth floating high above our heads. It was beautiful. But it was also a long, long way away.

"With the rocket fuel gone, we'll never get back," she said.

"Oh, no," I groaned.

"*AH-CHOOO!*"

Splat ah-choooed.

CHAPTER 5

Splat to the Rescue!

"**W**ait just a minute!" Mrs. Hooplesnort shouted. "That's it!"

"What's it?" I asked.

"Ah-chooo!"

Splat ah-choooed.

"Yes!" She pointed at Splat.

Splat pointed at himself.

"Ah-chooo?"

"YES!" Mrs. Hooplesnort repeated.

In a flash, she reached outside our rubber ducky space-raft. Then she grabbed a handful of moon dust and began

fling-ing

it into Splat's face. This caused my poor pooch to do even more

"Ah-chooo!"-ing.

She pointed his nose toward the back of the raft. Then she continued to

fling, fling, fling

even more dust into his face, causing him to

"Ah-chooo! Ah-chooo! Ah-chooo!"

even more.

Before we knew it, we were rising off the surface of the moon!

fling, fling, fling

"*Ah-chooo! Ah-chooo! Ah-chooo!*"

That's right! We'd gone from rocket power to sneeze power!

"Attaboy, Splat!" I shouted. "Keep it up!"

He nodded in agreement and kept on

"*Ah-chooo!*"-ing.

(Not that he had much choice with all of Mrs. Hooplesnort's *fling*-ing.)

Soon, we were heading back home! Home, sweet home.

Of course, it would have been a little

sweeter if all the countries hadn't started firing

ZING! ZING! ZING!

missiles at us!

"What are they doing?!" I shouted.

"Trying to shoot us down, Bernie!" Mrs. Hooplesnort yelled.

"WHAT?!"

"They must think we're invaders from another planet!"

"Oh, no!"

So, there we were, Mrs. Hooplesnort

fling, fling, fling-ing

as Splat was

"*AH-CHOOO! AH-CHOOO! AH-CHOOO!*"-ing

as the missiles were

ZING! ZING! ZING!-ing.

I couldn't see how it could get any scarier. Unfortunately, I'd soon find out.

Eventually, we were back in Earth's gravity.

The good news was, we made it past the missiles.

The bad news was, we were falling faster than Dad's smile when he sees my three sisters' cell-phone bills.

"What do we do?!" Mrs. Hooplesnort shouted.

I didn't have a clue. But I did have my backpack.

I reached into it and pulled out a pair of—

"Earmuffs?!" Mrs. Hooplesnort shouted. "What are we supposed to do with earmuffs?!"

I stared at them and shrugged. "Wear them to keep our ears warm?" I gave a weak smile.

She didn't smile back.

Splat grabbed them and plopped them on his ears. (I guess he likes toasty ears.)

Suddenly, we heard:

"AGENT DINGLEDORF!
AGENT DINGLEDORF!"

We looked at the ducky raft's dashboard. There was a TV picture of—

"Big Guy!" I shouted.

"Secret Agent Dingledorf," he said.

"Don't come to Headquarters. We haven't the time!"

"What's going on?" I shouted.

"It's the boys at B.A.D.D.," he said.

"B.A.D.D.?" Mrs. Hooplesnort asked.

I turned to her and explained, "**B**ungling **A**gents **D**edicated to **D**estruction."

Big Guy continued. "They're trying to take over the world."

"Again?" I sighed. "What is it this time?"

A picture of a rock band appeared on the screen. They were older guys. The singer had hair frizzier than cotton candy—and just as pink.

"This is a new music group called 'Too Weird,'" Big Guy said. "B.A.D.D. broadcasts their music through a machine called 'The Brain Wave Mixer Upper.'"

"And that's bad?" I asked.

"I'll say," Mrs. Hooplesnort said. "Just

look at that hair!"

"Not only that," Big Guy said, "but when children hear their music, they do crazy things."

"Like what?"

"It makes them forget how their bodies work. They start using them in weird ways."

As Big Guy spoke, we got closer to Earth. And, as we got closer, I could hear the music again.

"How do we stop them?" asked Mrs. Hooplesnort.

"A good question. First, you must go to the radio station where they're broadcasting and . . ."

As the music grew louder, Big Guy's voice grew fainter.

For some reason, I raised my feet closer to the speaker so I could hear better.

". . . then you must find a way to convince the band to stop playing . . ."

His voice continued fading.
I kicked off my shoes and peeled off my socks to better listen.

". . . through the Brain Wave Mixer Upper, and . . ."

I shoved my toes right up against the speaker.

". . . everything should turn backxxxxxxxxxxxxxxxxxxxxxxx

But that's all I heard. I saw Big Guy's lips moving, but that was it. No matter how hard I strained my toes to listen, the only thing they heard was:

Mrs. Hooplesnort turned to me and spoke.

I pointed my toes toward her. But, again, all I heard was:

Suddenly, I understood. "OH, NO!" I shouted. "IT'S MIXING MY BRAIN WAVES AGAIN!! WHAT DO I DO?!"

At least that's what I tried to shout. Unfortunately, it sounded more like

"BURPA-BURP!"
"BURPA-BURP BURP BURP!"

Which, as you already know, is the sound you make when talking with your armpit!

CHAPTER 6

The Race Is On!

So, there we were . . . falling a gazillion miles an hour . . . screaming, barking, and, of course, *"Burpa-Burpa-Burp"*-ing for our lives.

Now was the time we needed a hero.

Now was the time for Splat to prove his incredible wonder-doggieness.

Unfortunately, it was also the time for him to climb on top of my head, tremble in fear, and

"Whimper, whimper, whimper."

"Burp!" I shouted. *"Burpa-Burp!"*

(*Translation:* "Splat! Get down!")

But Splat was in no mood to get down.

He was only in the mood for clinging to my head and whimpering.

Fortunately, when he clung to my head, he also covered my ears.

And covering my ears meant I couldn't hear the music.

And not hearing the music meant . . . you guessed it, my brain suddenly cleared up!

"Splat!" I shouted. "You're a genius!"

He nodded bravely and

"whimper, whimper, whimper"-ed

some more.

Now there was just one other problem. The one of hitting the ground!

Any second, we'd crash into Earth harder

than my oldest sister hit that pickup on her first day of driving . . . or that bus on her second day . . . or that semitruck on her— well, you get the picture.

So did Mrs. Hooplesnort.

She quickly flung the rest of the moon dust into Splat's face.

Which meant he quickly traded in his

"whimper, whimper, whimper"-ing

for

"Ah-chooo! Ah-chooo! Ah-chooo!"-ing.

She pointed his nose to the ground. And, just as his allergy helped us take off from the moon, it now

"Ah-chooo! Ah-chooo! Ah-chooo!"

slowed down our falling.

In seconds, we landed.

Now we had to race to the radio station and stop Too Weird from playing their music.

But how?

I had no idea. (Which is how I solve all my cases. So I figured I was on the right track.)

As soon as we stepped out of the ducky raft it

K-shrink,
K-fold,
K-change, K-change, K-chang-ed

into a pair of Rollerblades.

I turned and saw Mrs. Hooplesnort running off in the opposite direction.

"Mrs. Hooplesnort!" I shouted. "The radio station is this way!"

"I know!" she yelled. "But school is over, and I haven't given any homework! How will they ever learn anything?"

I guess we all have priorities. For some it's saving the world. For others it's giving homework assignments.

But I still had Splat.

"Come on, boy!" I slipped into the Rollerblades and we took off. "We've got a world to save!"

"Whimper, whimper, whimper,"

he whimpered as he clung to my head, still covering my ears.

By now, Too Weird's music was blasting from every radio in town. And things

were worse than ever. . . .

Little guys on tricycles were pedaling with their hands.

Kids on scooters were pushing with their tongues. (Not a pretty sight . . . or taste.)

And Priscilla? When we passed her, she was still walking on her hands, and

she was still

Hic, Hic, Hic-cupp-ing!

through her ears.
    No doubt about it. We had to stop Too
Weird from playing any more music!

When we arrived at the radio station, B.A.D.D. agents were everywhere.

"Hey, kid!" One of them was waving. "You can't go into the party like that!"

I pulled Splat's paws from my ears and shouted, "What's wrong with me?"

"Exactly!" he shouted back.

"What?!"

"I see nothing wrong with you!"

"And that's wrong?"

He nodded. "If nothing's wrong with you, then everything is right with you—which means you're wrong for being right."

(Unfortunately, I understood perfectly.)

Without a word, I pulled off my Rollerblades and grabbed Splat's collar.

I slapped it around my neck and pulled a leash from my backpack. Then I handed the leash to Splat, dropped to all fours, and pretended to be *his* pet.

"That's better!" the man shouted.

"Because it's wrong?" I asked.

"That's right!"

I nodded and reached for the earmuffs Splat had been wearing.

I put them on my own ears, and we headed inside.

CHAPTER 7

Too Weird

The room was packed with kids. Some were clapping with their elbows. Others were trying to eat with their bellybuttons. Others just stood upside down on their shoulders and listened.

I walked over to the punch bowl. "This is too weird!" I shouted to Splat.

"No!" One of the kids yelled and pointed to the band. "That's Too Weird over there!"

I turned toward the stage. The band was a bunch of older guys. They had the same guitars, keyboard, and drums as any other band. But all their speakers pointed toward a giant machine.

"That must be the Brain Wave Mixer Upper!" I shouted to Splat.

"Whimper,"

he whimpered back.

"We've got to tell them what they're doing!" I yelled.

"Whimper, whimper,"

he whimpered.

Without a word (but plenty more whimpering), Splat crawled back up to my shoulders and we headed for the band.

I got the attention of the singer with the pink hair. "Why are you doing this?" I shouted.

He yelled, "What?"

I pointed at the machine in front of

them. "Why are you using the Brain Wave Mixer Upper?" I shouted. "Why are you making kids' bodies do weird things?"

I pulled off my earmuffs just long enough to hear his answer. "The fellows at B.A.D.D. said it would make things better!" he yelled.

"You call this 'better'?!" I shouted.

Pink Hair looked around. Every kid in the room was doing weird things with their bodies.

I remembered what Mrs. Hooplesnort had said in health class and shouted, "God made our bodies wonderful just the way they are! What makes you think you can make them better?!"

"But the boys at B.A.D.D. said—"

"Don't listen to them!" I shouted. "They just want to take over the world!"

Suddenly, a B.A.D.D. guard appeared.

"What's wrong?" he yelled.

"Nothing is wrong!" Pink Hair shouted.

(Which, as we know from the last chapter, is the wrong answer.)

"That's what I thought!" the guard yelled. He motioned to a couple more B.A.D.D. guys and they started for us.

I had to think of some way to stop them.

Of course, I also had to think of some way not to wind up in the hospital.

Decisions, decisions. Would it be:

A. Save the world, and be a dead hero.
B. Run for my life, and be a live chicken.

I hate multiple-choice questions, don't you?

I turned to Splat for his opinion. (I don't want to say Wonder-dog is a coward, but if he looked any more chicken, he'd be sprouting feathers, flapping his wings, and clucking.)

For him, it was definitely time to run. Swiftly, he leaped from my shoulders.

Actually, it wasn't so swift. And it wasn't much of a leap.

Instead, it was more of a

"W
h
i   w
m   h
p   i   w
e   m   h
r   p   i
       e   m
       r   p
             e
             r"

fall.

Straight down . . .

Straight onto the control panel of the Brain Wave Mixer Upper . . .

Straight onto the little button that read:

WARNING

Press to control the whole world.

(This means adults, too!)

And, just like that, the music started affecting grown-ups also.

Suddenly, the B.A.D.D. guys flipped onto their heads. I saw them trying to shout with their hipbones—threatening to beat me up with their earlobes.

Then there was the band.

Not only were they using their bodies wrong, but also their instruments.

Suddenly, the drummer began drumming his kneecaps.

The piano player started playing his teeth.

And the guitarist? Somebody tossed him a caramel apple. But he didn't catch it. Instead, he swung his guitar at it like a baseball bat and

K-SPLEWIE . . .

pieces of broken apple flew across the crowd.

"Watch it!" someone shouted. He picked up a handful of pretzels and threw them back at the band.

Somebody else yelled, "Knock it off!" and threw a meatball.

Someone else threw a glass full of punch.

And, before you know it, the whole party had turned into a food fight.

You name it, it was flying . . . popcorn,

chips (complete with dip), slices of pizza (complete with extra sauce).

But they weren't thrown the usual way.

Instead, someone was

poof . . . ping
poof . . . ping
poof . . . ping

shooting peanuts out his nose.

Someone else had dipped her hair into the punch bowl and was

fling, fling, fling-ing

it around, spraying everybody.

Then there was the kid with bare feet. He'd greased his soles with ketchup and when he clapped them together he could *squirt, squirt, squirt*

those little smoked sausage thingies
halfway across the room.

I turned to Pink Hair and shouted,
"What do we do?!"

But he was too busy throwing salsa
and ducking from

splat, splat, splat

exploding Twinkies being launched from
someone's mouth.

Things were definitely worse in a not-
so-good way!

CHAPTER 8

The Case Closes

So, there we were. Every man, woman, and child was controlled by the Brain Wave Mixer Upper.

There was no one to help. Not a single human being could . . .

Wait a minute.

It was true, there was no *human* who could help.

But what about a brown, pudgy, four-legged Super-dog?!

I spun around and searched the room.

"Splat!" I called. "Splat, where are you?!"

And then I spotted him. He was scampering across the floor, gobbling up all the food he could find. Chips, dip, hot dogs. You name it, he was gobbling it.

"Splat!" I shouted. "Splat!"

He heard me and stopped eating.

"This is your chance to be a hero!" I shouted. "You can save the day!"

He looked at me, gave a loud

BURP,

and returned to his gobbling.

(Like I said, everybody has their priorities.)

But there had to be some way to get him to help. Some way to—and then I spotted it:

About five feet off the floor, above a chair, was an outlet.

An electric cord that connected the band's speakers was plugged into it.

An electric cord that had a nice piece

of oozing, greasy pizza dripping from it.

"Splat!" I pointed. "Up there! See the cord? See the nice, oozing, greasy pizza dripping from it?"

He did. Faster than you can say "doggie garbage disposal," he raced to the chair. After several tries, he finally climbed on top of it.

But the oozing, greasy pizza was still several feet above him. He began

"BARK! BARK!"-ing
and
jump, jumping.

Lots of

"BARK! BARK!"-ing
and
jump, jumping

until, finally, he

"*BARK! BARK!*"-ed,
jumped, jumped,
and
CHOMP, CHOMP-ed

down on the pizza.

The only problem was, he was so busy *chomp, chomp*-ing, he forgot about the fall, falling.

Which he did. Right on his head.

The good news was, when he fell, he pulled out the cord and unplugged the speakers.

The bad news was, he'd also unplugged his brain.

That's right. The poor fellow landed on his head and knocked himself out.

"SPLAT!" I yelled.

I raced to his side.

"SPLAT!"

I took his head into my hands and shouted, "SPEAK TO ME, LITTLE FELLOW! SPEAK TO ME!"

People gathered around us.

"SPLAT!"

Then, ever so slowly, he opened one eye.

"YOU'RE ALIVE!" I shouted. "SPEAK TO ME! SAY SOMETHING! SAY ANY-THING!"

He opened his mouth.

I leaned forward to better hear. "ANY-THING!" I said.

He took a deep breath.

"ANYTHING AT ALL!"

And then he let out the world's longest and loudest

BUUUURRRP . . .

(I guess I did say "*anything*.")

Pink Hair bent down to join us. "Is he going to be all right?"

"I think so," I said.

He nodded and looked out over the crowd. Everybody was back on their feet. Everybody was remembering how to use their bodies. And, by the looks of things, everybody was a lot happier.

"Hey, you!"

He turned to see one of the B.A.D.D. agents approaching and shouting, "Get back to playing that music."

Pink Hair rose to his feet and shook his head. "I don't think so."

"What do you mean? Without your music, our Brain Wave Mixer Upper won't work."

Pink Hair nodded. "And by the looks of things, that's how it should be."

"But we won't be able to take over the world. Kids will start using their bodies the old-fashioned way."

"Which is how it should be," Pink Hair said.

"But—"

"God made our bodies wonderful just the way they are!"

"But, but—"

"What makes you think we can improve them?" Pink Hair looked down at me and gave a wink.

Then, turning to the rest of his band, he called, "Come on, guys. Let's get out of here."

And so the party came to an end.

The music had stopped.

The kids had returned to normal.

And Splat? He was still a little woozy. But he noticed a pizza cheese puddle on the floor near his face. He wasn't strong enough to move, but he was strong enough to stretch out his tongue and

slurp-slurp-slurp

it up.

Which, of course, he did.

Which, of course, led to one more

BURP!

Which, of course, was just fine with me.

By the next day, things were pretty much back to normal.

My three sisters were back to their normal weirdness:

". . . Johnny is, like, soooo cute, and . . ."

". . . told Melvin who told Melissa to tell Mary to tell . . ."

". . . but I just wore this skirt three months ago . . ."

And, of course, Splat was back to his normal weirdness. (At the moment that meant being a doggie vacuum cleaner— sniffing and snorting under the break- fast table for any fallen crumbs.)

Heading off to school was pretty nor- mal, too.

"Hey, Bernie *(sniff-sniff)*, wait up!"

I turned to see I.Q. and Priscilla run- ning to catch up. The good news was, they were running on their feet.

The bad news was, Priscilla was rubbing her fist.

"What's wrong with your hand?" I asked.

"She sprained it on Jimmy Snodgrass's face," I.Q. explained.

I turned to her. "He didn't tell you that you're pretty again?"

"Yeah." She sighed. "Some guys never learn."

Yes sir, things were definitely back to normal.

They were even back to normal in Mrs. Hooplesnort's class.

"Class, I'm so sorry I wasn't here to give you all your homework yesterday."

Everyone nodded, pretending to be sad.

"To make it up to you," she said, "I have a special homework assignment for the weekend."

Suddenly, we didn't have to pretend to be sad.

"That's right." She smiled. "And if you're lucky, it will only take all of Saturday and most of Sunday."

Everyone

GROAN-ed.

Well, everyone but Raymond the human rash.

Instead of groaning, he thought it would be funny to talk like he did yesterday. So he shoved his hand under his armpit and started with the

"burpa-burpa-burpa-burpa"-s

again.

And he was right. It was funny. Especially the part where Mrs. Hooplesnort yanked him out of his chair and sent him to the office.

"Now, where was I?" she asked.

"Something about *(sniff-sniff)* destroying our weekend?" I.Q. said.

Mrs. Hooplesnort nodded. "That's right. I want you to write something about the human body and just how wonderfully it's made."

There were even louder

GROAN-s

She continued. "It can be a poem or an essay or . . . even a true story."

She looked at me and grinned. (Well, I thought it was a grin. Sometimes it's hard to tell with Mrs. Hooplesnort.)

But it made no difference. I knew it

wouldn't take long to write. After all, I'd already—

beep-beep-beep-beep

What was I saying? Oh, yeah—since I had already lived the story, I knew it wouldn't take long to write it.

beep-beep-beep-beep

And a good thing, too. Because the way my underwear continued to

beep-beep-beep-beep,

it sounded like I was about to start another mission.

And, if that was true, I'd need all the time I could

beep-beep-beep-beep

get.

That's right. While some kids have their weekend soccer games or ballet lessons or whatever . . . I have to do secret agent stuff like saving the world.

But that's okay with me. The way I figure it, everybody needs a little

beep-beep-beep-beep

hobby.

Look for These Other Books in This Series

The Case of the Giggling Geeks

The world's smartest people can't stop laughing. Is this the work of the crazy criminal Dr. Chuckles? Only Secret Agent Dingledorf (the country's greatest agent, even though he is just ten years old) can find out. Together, with super cool inventions (that always backfire), major mix-ups (that become major mishaps), and the help of Splat the Wonder-dog, our hero winds up saving the day . . . while discovering the importance of respecting and loving others.

ISBN 1-4003-0094-0

www.tommynelson.com

A Division of Thomas Nelson, Inc.
www.ThomasNelson.com

The Case of the Chewable Worms

The earth is being invaded by worms! They're everywhere . . . crawling on kid's toothbrushes, squirming in their sandwiches. And worst of all, people find them . . . tasty! But is it really an invasion or the work of B.A.D.D. (Bungling Agents Dedicated to Destruction)? Only Secret Agent Dingledorf and his trusty dog, Splat, can find out and save the day . . . while also realizing the importance of doing good and helping others.   ISBN 1-4003-0095-9

www.tommynelson.com

A Division of Thomas Nelson, Inc.
www.ThomasNelson.com